Jasmine

A Woman of Color

UP AND COMING BEST SELLER AUTHOR

Jasmine
A Woman of Color

ML BOYD

ReadersMagnet, LLC

Contents

The Marriage

I FINALLY FOUND AND MARRIED MY soul mate and the love of my life. I had been to the point in my life that I was convinced that I would be a single parent for the rest of my life until Mike came along. Mike Moore was my strong warrior that gave me strength and confidence where I had lost it somewhere in my life, or so I thought.

Both Mike and I had a child each, we had been raising them as single parents. I was sure that I was the happiest that I had ever been. I had no clue just how much things would change in our married life until a year later. I was 10 years Mike's Jr., when Mike and I got married our sex life was very good and active but something changed along the way.

Year 1 ~ I was still in blest but something has changed in our life. I started to notice how Mike was no longer romantic he stopped sending roses, or taking me out to dinner. I started to notice how Mike was not talking to me anymore but would spend more time on the internet talking to females on line.

"Mike can we talk?"

"What do you want to talk about Jas?"

"Well I want us to do something romantic or something special, we haven't done anything in a while so how about going out to eat?"

"Well I really don't feel up to it, maybe some other night it really is not a good time right now. It is not a necessity to go out to eat or go and do something together".

I walked away with tears in my eyes and went into the kitchen to make dinner. I found myself crying increasingly every day. I began to do what made me feel better so I thought if I did not have the extra money to buy things, I ate. I started to notice that my clothes where starting not to fit any more, and my dress size was going from a size six to a size eight.

I found myself keeping busy with my full time job and trying to run a part time cosmetic business from home. I know in the back of my mind that something was wrong with my marriage but Mike was not helping me fix the problems he started to ignore me at every turn. Mike stopped making love to me unless I made it an issue. I found myself extremely unhappy at every turn except for when I worked my cosmetic business for one of the largest cosmetics business in the world or worked at my full time job. I began to eat even more to the point I increased my dress size to a twelve.

I started to see changes in Mike and his reactions when our daughters and I were around him and his laptop. Mike would smile at the computer screen as if he was having a conversation with someone that he wanted to be with instead of me. Mike would always lower his screen so that no one could see what he was working on or put up his hand up to shield the screen, and whom he is talking too. One day at work while on my lunch break I heard a voice, that said for me to look on-line in the personal section. To my dismay, I found that Mike had placed an ad. I started to cry not believing my eyes.

My worst fears had come true my husband is cheating on me or trying too. I read his ad "I am not wanting, to interfere or cause problems if you're married. I'm looking for a female friend on-line internet companionship or in person missing something in my own marriage."

Out of heartache decided to place an ad of my own. I did not want to have an affair, but just to get back at Mike in one way or another. Even placing an ad I knew in my heart that I would not cheat. My heart broken and wondering, what did I do wrong to cause my husband to have an affair and to place an ad in the personal section? I started to wonder was it the weight that I had gained in the last year to cause Mike to look elsewhere. Was I bad in bed? I remembered a time that Mike had told me that I was the best that he had ever had especially when it came to sucking his dick. So what had changed? I wanted to know if I was still attractive to men. What was it about me that caused Mike to look elsewhere? I was sure if I confronted him he would turn it back around to me. He never excepted blame or being wrong of anything. Mike is a manipulator and controlling he is a master at it.

Was I that bad looking was I that bad of a wife and mother? I started to fall into a deep depression that I knew that I had to get out of and the only way out of it was to fight. I refused to go on an anti-depression I wanted to fix what was wrong in my life and my marriage.

I thought that maybe if I would give things time that things would change. I decided to ask Mike one day why he did not want to make love to me. Mike's answer surprised me "I'm just going through the midlife crises, my desire is just low right now" I loving my husband and wanting to belief him accepted this answer. Just give it time I told myself. "Ok Mike what can I do to help, have you thought about going to the doctor and seeing what can be done?" "No and I'm not going to I don't want to take anything." "Fine then." I walk to our bedroom to have a good cry in the bathroom.

I was sure that he was having an affair with a woman named Betsy someone he met online. The time before her, other women named Sharon, Pat and Marcia. Of course, I had no proof about Betsy just my feeling something was not right with this relationship. Everything pointed to an affair. She calls the house and if I answered, she hangs up the phone, then calls and text messages on his phone. Mike disappears for hours at a time to run errands. Mike refusing to join me on any trips I would have to take. Mike stopped giving me gifts for Christmas, our anniversary or any special occasions.

I was feeling unappreciated, un-loved and lonelier by the day. I was emotionally eating all the time whenever I was around Mike, so much so that I went from a size eight to a size twelve in less than 3 months it seemed like. Then before I knew it, I was wearing a size fourteen. Now to my surprise I am now wearing a size sixteen.

Anytime old friends saw me, they were shocked at how much weight I had gained. I had taken all of the teasing and cruel words by some. Some I found did not say anything but gave me support and understanding from the weight gain for they too had the same problem.

While I continued to emotionally eat and live, day-by-day Mike continued to push me further away. Mike was a master of cruel words and ignoring me. I found comfort with my friends, and the men at work, they would give me compliments even with the added weight I still took pride in how I looked and would always dress for success. I wondered how I could receive plenty of compliments from my coworkers, and men that worked in the company but not from my own husband. I even asked my dear old friend Jack what was wrong with my and what's I doing wrong.

"Jasmine you're doing nothing wrong you are a wonderful and extraordinary woman and don't you forget that. If I was younger and not married I would have asked you out myself." "I've seen the way men look at you and believe me that you make men's heads turn hard." "Jack your biased you are my brother you're going to say that and I love you for it."

"Jack it is so hard to believe because of Mike's response to me especially at night." I need to know that my husband loves me and wants to be with me."

"Jasmine, you will be fine I want you to be strong and you know that you will always have my shoulder to lean on. I always knew that Mike had to be special and in love with you in order for you to marry him."

"Jack thanks for the ear I needed to talk to a man to see what I'm doing wrong as a wife and mother."

"Jasmine you have to stop blaming yourself and finding fault with yourself for something your husband is not doing. Mike is the one with the problem not you."

Year 10 ~ I finally realize that Mike will never change and is unwilling to help make our marriage work. I still did not have complete proof that Mike has been cheating on me all of these years and I've decided to let go of trying to make Mike happy. It is past time to make me happy from the inside out. I truly believe that it is not my looks or love making that is the problem. I am convinced more now than ever it is my weight that is part of the problem and the other part is Mike.

I have been working on finishing my Business Management degree with a minor in Communication. Now I am so close in finishing it just two more classes and I will be graduating. My boss Adam told me how proud he is of me working to complete my degree and when I graduate, he would give me a pay raise. I was thrilled I enjoyed working with Adam. Adam has a wonderful fun personality at least the side I see at work, his wife is so lucky.

The Funeral

I SAT WITH THE REST OF the family members at my grandfather's funeral. I could not belief that he was gone. We had a wonderful relationship; I was his only grandchild with the exception of my daughter and his only child my mother had already died years ago. My great grandfather had passed away when I was 3 years old and then his mother passed when I was 16. My grandfather Bobby had three brothers and two sisters, with only one sister, and two brothers still living.

The second oldest brother had called me 5 nights ago, 1:00 in the morning saying my grandfather had passed away. They took him to the hospital around 9:00 after a late dinner they had together. He had complained about chest pains. The doctors and nurses worked hard with him but he had another heart attack came and Bobby passed around 11:00.

My great uncle told me that Bobby had left instructions with his lawyer to contact me that his insurance policy would handle all of the funeral arrangements and to fly me, and my family out. When I told Mike he said for me to go ahead and fly out with the girls and he would stay behind. I felt very hurt that Mike would not go to be with me and to give me comfort at this time but I took it and moved on.

Two days after my grandfather's death Lexus, Michelle and I had flew to Dallas, Texas for the funeral that was 3 days away. I spent time helping my family and got ready for the funeral. I received a call from my grandfather's attorney the day after I arrived, told me that he needed to have a private word with me after the funeral, and would like to pick me up and take me to his office. I asked Mr. Stokes what was this about, and the only thing he would tell me is that it is about your grandfather's will. I agreed for us to meet after the funeral.

The day of the funeral, I was extremely upset. I felt like I was losing my very best friend. I remembered all the times that I would be thinking about him and he would call me or vs. versa. Bobby and I were close and we had many laughs. Bobby would fly me out to visit whenever I wanted to come and assisted me several times when I needed money.

Now he was gone and I could not believe it. No more calls every 2 weeks. After the funeral, Mr. Stokes showed up as promised and took me and my great uncles and aunt away to his office. My daughters where taken back to the house first. Mr. Stokes began with the normal reading of the will. Bobby had a nice large insurance policy that he split evenly among his brothers and sisters.

Jasmine your grandfather has left you a trust fund that he started years ago when you were a little girl and when you had your daughter he had started one for her as well.

"Jasmine the trust fund is for you to do with as you please, and your daughter's trust fund has provisions, between you and I will monitor. Basically she must finish college, when she turns 35 then she may have the trust fund to do with as I please only if you and I are in agreement as too her being responsible enough to handle it. I looked at Mr. Stokes and agreed. Mr. Stokes asked the others to leave the room per Bobby's instructions."

Once the others had left, Mr. Stokes informed me of just how much money was in my trust fund.

"Jasmine your grandfather was a rich man he did not have to want for anything. Your grandfather was always putting money into your trust fund and now the fund is a little over five million dollars. This is not including the other property and money that is part of his estate that he left you as well." My head was spinning from what Mr. Stokes was telling me.

"Are you kidding me Mr. Stokes because if you are I am not in any mood to be the punch line of a joke"?

"Mrs. Moore I assure you that this is no joke you now have full control of your trust fund to do with it as you please and you need to decide what you would like to do with your grandfather's estate. I will be more than willing to assist you with anything. Your grandfather has already taken care of my legal fees before he passed and set up an account for all of my legal services that you may need for the next year."

"Mr. Stokes I'm very overwhelmed by what you are telling me and I need time to understand all of this. Please tell me what is in my grandfather's estate."

"Well as you know he always lived in an apartment but he made wise investments and he sold all of his real estate property just a few months ago while the market was hot. Therefore, you also have in addition to your trust fund another 1 million dollars from the sale of the real estate that he had not moved into any kind of investments at the time. Then you have all of his mature cd's that he had another 2 million that you're the beneficiary of and then you have his regular bank accounts savings 2 million and he always had one hundred thousand dollars in his checking account."

"Mr. Stokes I'm really in shock and well what is it that you need me to do?"

"Well right now I will give the bank a copy of the death certificate and we will have you sign some bank papers."

"Mr. Stokes can I leave the money right where it is and draw money from the accounts?"

"Yes but do you want me to transfer money into your checking account in Kansas?" '(Say no, say no)' "No Mr. Stokes I would just like to leave the money where it is but I would like to transfer eight thousand dollars to my joint account with my husband for now. Then I would like for you to transfer twenty thousand into my business account and four thousand in traveler's checks or a debt gift card."

"Ok Mrs. Moore I will do anything you ask."

Two hours later I was still shaking from shock, I had no idea that my grandfather had all of that money.

"Good Mr. Stokes something is telling me to keep this information to myself for now I don't want to tell my husband or kids."

"Mrs. Moore do you have time right now to go to the bank around the corner? It is the main bank for your grandfather's account." "Yes Mr. Stokes." One hour later, we came out of the bank.

I told Mr. Stokes before I left his office to donate all of my grandfather's clothes to a homeless shelter. I also had a ten thousand dollar cashier's check made out to the local women's shelter in my grandfather's name Mr. Stokes promised to get it delivered.

I sat thinking about how the soft voice that has helped guide me over the years told me to say no about transferring the money into their account. I learned a long time ago to trust and do whatever that soft voice said. It was always right even if I did not completely understand at that time the reason I felt that God would let me know when the time was right.

So far, God has won out every time. So for now I will keep the money a secret for as long as I can and if Mike asks me where did the money come from then I will tell him that my grandfather left me the money and that would be the truth but I won't say just how much he left me.

Later that night I called Mike to tell him goodnight but there was no answer at our home number or his cell phone. Strange I thought he said that he would be home all night. I went to bed with a feeling of unease.

The next day I drove about 45 minutes outside of Dallas to Harsboro to the Prime Outlet Mall that I liked to shop at whenever I traveled to Dallas. When I drive to Dallas, I always stop at the Prime Outlet Mall in Gainesville, which is about 1 hour north of Dallas just off I-35. If we do not find anything in Harsboro, then I go to hit the malls in Dallas.

Five hours later, we all walked into the hotel room laughing. My daughters and I had a good time we were able to get away for a little bit and have some fun. I had forgotten some of my deep down troubles and worries for a little bit. Still puzzled over my angels message to 'say

No don't transfer all of the money.' Not knowing why but I will accept it for now and wait for the answers to come.

Two days later my daughters and I were flying back home. I found myself very tired and wanting to take a few extra days off from work to recoup. I called my boss Adam about taking a few extra days off. Adam was wonderful to me and said that it would be ok to take as much time off as I needed and to just call and keep him posted.

I told my daughters to go back to college the next day. I had called my college advisor a few days later asking her about what master programs where available to start taking if I find what I is looking for. I had worked extremely hard the last 6 years to get my degree in business management part-time while working a full time job and running my business.

3 Months Later

"JASMINE I'M GOING CAMPING THIS weekend if you don't mind?" "Oh I guess not Mike I have a wedding party to do the makeup for this weekend. So I will be tied up all day Saturday and I have a facial on Sunday."

"Ok I plan to be home around 5:00 pm on Sunday evening, I'm going to my usual spot."

"Ok Mike, when will you leave to go to the lake?" "I would like to leave no later than 5:00 pm Friday evening; I'm taking the boat so I can get out and fish." "Well I will be able to see you before you leave when I get off work tomorrow?" "Yep."

The next day I hurried home so I could say goodbye to Mike before he leaft. I was looking forward to having the house to myself so that I could get ready for the wedding on Saturday and the facial that I have to do on Sunday.

I was proud of myself with the way the bride, six bridesmaids, the mother of the bride and mother of the groom's makeup came out. I had all of them done on time. I had promised the bride that I would be around for the whole wedding and the pictures to touch up their makeup. I left the reception after I did the last touch up on the bride's makeup after she changed into another dress before leaving the wedding.

I came home very tired but thrilled that I picked up three more brides to do their weddings. My business was increasing each day. I believe that it is due to the Prayer of Jabez that I have been saying. God has been increasing my territory each day.

I unloaded my makeup travel bag glad that I had packed extra colors because of some of the last minute emergencies at a wedding. I walked into the house turning off the alarm and turning on the lights went down the hallway to my office. I went into the newly decorated room, and put down my bags and took out my smart phone to hot sink with my laptop. I thought about how wonderful my office turned out and how organized I felt.

I had turned the bedroom into my office once Michelle went to college. I had taken the time to find what I wanted for office furniture that would fit the room since it was so small. I was thrilled with the results I got; I found a nice corner L shaped workspace. In addition, a lateral file cabinet, and a desk, which I was not sure if I could get all the pieces in the room at first.

I put the corner unit into the corner on the right and from that the desk is angled just enough that I have plenty of room to come around the desk. I found a lovely little vanity table and had a nice size mirror added to the wall with a good wall mounted glamour lights above so that I can do facials there in the office. I had turned the closet into a real nice organized shelving unit to hold all of my supplies in order to hold all of my in stock items.

The last two touches I had added to the room that was very important was a small area rug and two nice u shaped chairs. I accented the room with purple, lavender, and soft pastel jade and nice neutral taupe's. This was my room that I found serenity and peace of mind in, Mike rarely came in this room.

I put everything away and sat down in the chair across from my desk and removed my shoes which my feet where killing me. Just then, the doorbell rang. I was thinking that I could not belief that someone was at my door. I was not expecting anyone. It could be one of the women that I gave a business card to but I doubt it. Usually they would just call but I did have one or two that have just dropped by.

I went to the door and was thankful I remembered to lock the screen door when I came in. There were two police officers standing there. "Yes." "Are you Mrs. Moore?"

"Yes officer." "Do you mind if we come in and talk to you Mrs. Moore?" "Ok but what is this about." I unlocked and opened the door and the two officers came in.

"Well Mrs. Moore would you please sit down we need to talk to you about a Mike Moore."

"Mike what about Mike?"

"Mrs. Moore your husband was out at Eldorado Lake in his boat fishing early this morning before other boats where out on the water. Someone saw your husband fall out of the boat and into the lake. He never re-surfaced. The witness was too far away and did not have a boat to go out but did contact the park rangers. We have combed the area and we have not found his body yet."

"Oh my God. Are you sure officer?" "Yes, we found his jacket in the boat with his id card in it. Mrs. Moore can you please tell us why you where not with him?"

"Yes. I had a bridal party to do their makeup for the wedding this afternoon in fact, I just got back a few minutes ago and I have a facial scheduled for tomorrow, so I told Mike to go ahead and have fun. I really don't like camping that much."

"Ok Mrs. Moore I will tell you that we are doing everything that we can but so far we have not found your husband. If we do not find your husband's body by tomorrow we will pronounce him dead." 'Dead he said the word dead.' "Mrs. Moore, do you have anyone to come and stay with you?"

"Yes I think so; I have to call my two daughters they're at college." "What colleges do we attend?"

"Michelle is at KU and Lexus is at K State, then I can call one of my best friends and I'm sure they will come over to stay with me."

"Is there anyone that could drive your daughters' home from school?" "I'm sure that I could get one of their friends to it and if not one of mine would be able to go get them." "Ok Mrs. Moore here is a number that you can call and check on the status of the search."

Three days later I was told that the search for my husband was being called off we were going to call my husband dead body missing. I called all the family members that needed to be called and told them what the status was on Mike. Everyone rallied around my two daughters and me.

I had plenty of help to arrange the funeral service for Mike. My best girlfriends all came running when I called. I was grateful that we all had that kind of friendship with each other.

The Truth

I HAD SUSPECTED MY HUSBAND OF having an affair but when I confronted him, he denied everything. I wanted to believe him and prayed that he was faithful, but he was not and never was. I always tried to keep our marriage exciting asked him to spend time together. Now I knew why he always had an excuse not to, or it was his job. Now that I thought about it, he had even stopped saying I love you back to my or even stop saying it at all. Even when I said it to him, he would reply I know you do, mm hmm or give my no response at all. Or how he would always would return to his old habits after 3-6 months to hiding his screens again like he is just looking at a web page. Mike thinks I am stupid and don't see what he's doing. Fine let him think that. It just confirms what I already know.

I found out about my husband cheating after his death. When I finally got the strength up to pack up all of his things away. That's when I found all of the ex-rated tapes and dvd's, receipts for hotel rooms in town none of which he shared with my. I tried to log onto Mike's computer but it was password protected as well as his instant messaging. I tried several attempts at a password protected and decided to get a hold of a computer geek at one of the colleges to break the code. Lexus was able to find someone that is good at hacking into a computer.

I found pictures of other women and him together, letters from several ladies to Mike saying how we enjoyed their time together.

How could he, how could he do this to me to our marriage? I fell to the floor on my knees crying, feeling totally betrayed and used. Oh if he were alive I would kill him no that would be too good for him. I would like to have tied him up and skinned him alive starting with his balls.

All of the times I suspected and he denied them; things would change for long periods of time then all over again. I realized that Mike would have always be the same if he had remained alive. How my heart hurts, now I knew what my mother meant when I said "I've' cried enough tears that tears won't fall from my eyes any longer but my heart cries."

That's it I've been hurt and betrayed by too many men. This time I'm going to do the hurting I thought. ("But that is not who you are my daughter") It is right now lord I'm sorry I'm hurting too much right now.

I called the only one person that could give my some support my best friend that was like a sister to my Diane. Diane was at my house in less than one hour. Diane sat in disbelief on what I had just told and showed her.

I told Diane that I did not know what I would have done if Mike were still alive and I had found out about this. "Jasmine you don't have to worry about that now Mike is dead. Start living your life you deserve it. Mike doesn't deserve your tears or your pity, move on with your life. You are one beautiful, smart woman and you deserve to be happy don't worry about that sorry son-of-a- bitch."

Diane sat with me for another hour and told me if I needed her to call.

After Diane left I was so damned angry a plan started forming in my mind. I got up and went to my desk began writing down names, and my plan formed to cause pain. I knew that I had the money to be able to carry out my plans. If he were alive, he would pay too.

When Mike died I received a nice size insurance policy on him and when my grandfather passed away three months before Mike and Bobby had left me a trust fund that was set-up years ago that had grown to the sum of five million dollars plus. Funny I thought Mike did not even attend the funeral with me in Texas and when the lawyer told me that he needed to talk to me before I left town I thought nothing of it.

I can remember my mouth had fallen open when the lawyer told me about the trust fund Bobby had left me. The strangest thing even more I thought I had not even told Mike when I returned. Now I sit and wonder why I had not told him about the money.

Then just 1 week later after Mike's memorial I bought one hundred dollars of lottery tickets just for fun and won another 60 million dollars. So yes, I had enough money to make everyone pay for the pain we caused me. My luck has turned around and it is time to make myself happy in the process. (Revenge will get you nowhere my child). Maybe not lord but I need a way to let go and I want others to own the pain they've caused. (It won't make you happy in the end. Revenge is just a temporary fix for you. Put your faith in me let me heal the pain). I'm sorry lord the pain is too great right now the hole too deep.

I decided to call a private investigator I interviewed several PI's before I decided on Gary Tyler to help me and my cause. I gave Gary a list of names and last known names about of eight people. Gary looked at the list of names I had provided.

"These women that you have listed what do you want to know about them." "Everything, marital statuses, who are their husbands, where they both work at, income, kids you name it. If they are married or have a significant other I want to know their routines, if they travel, go to the gym and I want pictures of anything interesting. If they are single do they have a boyfriend, and I want to same information on them."

"What about the men listed on your list?" "I want the same information on them. I want to know everything all routines with pictures."

"Ok Ms. Moore this will not going to be cheap to say the least, traveling expenses will have to be paid." "Look Mr. Tyler as long as you don't travel 1st class, and stay in the most expensive hotels the cost is not an issue to me. Just give me an accounting of all expenses, and tell me what your base rate is to start work on this?"

"Well Ms. Moore just to start off I need five thousand dollars, plus any additional expenses that is unseen." "Fine Mr. Tyler here is a check for seven thousand dollars and there will be a bonus check as well if you get everything I ask for within six months."

"How do you want me to contact you?" "For now call my cell phone number, I will be leaving town this week for at least six months or longer. If you need to meet with me in person just let me know and I can fly in or you can come to me in Denver."

"I will be renting an apartment there for the time being until I find a house to buy." "Ok Ms. Moore I'm glad to have you as a client." "Good Mr. Tyler I will expect to hear weekly reports from you and as soon as I get to Denver and get moved in I will send you my address, phone & fax numbers."

"Can I ask why you want all of this information?" "It's called paybacks Mr. Tyler, paybacks for all of the hurt and pain they have caused." "Well I know not to cause you any pain, but what if I find out information to cause you more pain?" "Don't worry Mr. Tyler what you find out could not cause me anymore then what I've find out in the last few weeks."

After I left Mr. Tyler's office I called the real estate's office. "Did you find anything for me to look at?"

"Yes Ms. Moore I did, I found three luxury apartments with all of your requirements. Will you be able to come out and look at them?" "I will be able to leave tomorrow morning; I'm on my way to make my arrangements now. I hope to be on a morning flight, so can I see them tomorrow afternoon?" "Yes that will be great, just give me a call and I will come by your hotel and pick you up Ms. Moore."

"Thanks Miss Johnson oh before I forget do you know any good luxury car dealers in town? I'm looking to purchase a Mercedes or a Cadillac while I'm there and if the dealer has all of those brands that would be great." "I do, after we look at the apartments I can take you by the dealership."

"Are you sure you don't mind Miss Johnson I don't want to be too much trouble?" "I'm sure and please call me Michelle." "All right Michelle and thank you I will call you once I'm checked into my hotel room. Oh one more thing I will need resources to get the apartment completely furnished as well in a short amount of time, so if you also know any interior decorators.

Michelle thank you for all of your help I really do appreciate it. I look forward to meeting you tomorrow." "I look forward to tomorrow as well Ms. Moore. Bye! Bye!"

Ok with that done I went straight to my office and got on the phone to make my arrangements; old habits are hard to break even if you do have money. I decided to splurge instead of booking a flight on a major airline I contacted a private jet company. One hour later I had a contract for a private flight. I called the limo service that I used in the past for service tomorrow morning picking my up at home and at the airport.

Wow its nice having money for a change, I don't have worry about living paycheck to paycheck. My house and cars all paid off with the insurance money from my husband's death. With the money from my trust fund and lottery winnings, I can go and do anything I want to. I decided to use my lottery winnings and to not touch my trust fund. After I won the lottery I went in to Adam's office and told him that I won the lottery and was quitting my job.

I remembered telling Adam that I would stay through the day but would like to leave quietly without anyone knowing. I would pack up my things and take them home that night. Adam asked if I could stay through the end of the week until he could get a permanent assistant.

"Jasmine I'm happy you won the money but I'm sad to lose you as my assistant. Thank you for all of the years you stuck by me and how well you ran the office." "Thanks Adam I really enjoyed working with you, you are a wonderful boss and a good man. Give me a call when you decide to retire this place. I may have a job you could come work for me instead." "Funny Jasmine what kind of job would that be?" "Oh I don't know yet maybe my business manager or you could run a business I'm thinking about starting or buying. Who knows right now the possibilities are endless. Just remember if you get tired of this place call me ok." "Alright Jas I will keep you in mind just don't be a stranger ok." "Ok Adam I won't I will keep in touch."

Now I have the means of assisting my daughter and stepdaughter. I set-up the same kind of trust funds for them Bobby set up they can have at the age of 35. If I die before then and they will both have a college fund that they will have access to a lawyer I hired without the girls knowing that the money came from me.

Both think that a relative left them the money for college, but they cannot spend that money freely we have to go to college and the college is paid through the lawyer with anything else we need. When I won the lottery, I did not tell a sole except Adam I would not let the lottery commission to announce my name, which was the best thing I could have done.

Now with my plan in motion I still have a lot to do before leaving tomorrow for whatever period it will take. Thank God, the girls are away at college. I had better call them and tell them they can get a hold of me on my cell phone and that I will be traveling for work. They have no idea that I quit my job I am going to have to tell them one day but not now.

I decided to go shopping for some new clothes that I knew I needed but only for a short time. Right now I currently weighed 185 pounds, part of my plan was to lose 75 pounds, and drop from sizes sixteen/eighteen to a size four/six. Once I pick out an apartment, I will hire a chief to cook all of my daily meals. I also will get a personal trainer to work with me in my apartment/condo. I would like to get a three bedroom and turn one of the rooms into a work out room and the second bedroom into my office.

I would pick up all of my new office equipment once I decided on an apartment/condo. I knew I wanted something big and if I could not find it in an apartment/condo I would have to rent a house. But if I really like living there I would have to consider buying a house. However, in the meantime part of my plan is to lose the weight and exercise intensely before seeing the plastic surgeon. I've always been well gifted and did not need to have any increase to my breast but they could stand a lift. But the rest of my body could stand a whole body lift.

I want to fix the ridge of my nose from years of wearing glasses as a girl. Once I get the weight off to have all of the access skin removed and maybe lipo-suction if needed. Maybe to do something with my double chin and anything else that I will need to take care of.

I still feel young well I am young I AM ONLY 40. The other thing I want to change will be my hair color. I finally have my hair long again past my shoulders I want my hair to go from black to a light honey brown. Mike never wanted me to change my color before. Now I have the courage to change and do what I want to.

My goal is to look different and to be so beautiful that I could have any man I wanted to. The only thing is I promised myself not be used or to get married ever again. I refused to be the one that gets hurt but would gladly hurt the ones that has caused my so much pain and for my heart to break. (My child let me heal your pain and heal your heart. Let me show you what love feels and look like). My heart is too black and blue now lord, Mike took the love and caused me pain to the point of no recovery. Love is not pain and love is not hurting you but that is all I know. All I've ever had from men. I'm not ready to be loved the way you want to show me.

Once I get settled in Denver I will find the right people to help me make my changes. I finally finished packing and got ready for bed I would have a long busy day tomorrow and the next few days.

The next morning I felt pampered being picked up by a car service I felt extremely special splurging the way I did yesterday. I bought myself several new coordinating outfits and then my big purchase of the day was my Gucci, Coach, and Michael Korrs handbags, new wardrobe and luggage. I was in a beautiful purple pant suit with matching shoes; my makeup was complementing my outfit perfect like a professional model thanks to my owing my own business as an independent beauty consultant. Hmmm I will have to think about letting that go now. I no longer need the business but enjoy it. I will think about that later.

I felt 100% better once I was off the hour and forty-five minute flight from Kansas to Denver I hate heights but will get on a plane to fly. I was told the day before because of the security measures at the airport that the limo driver would meet my down at the luggage claim area with a sign.

One hour later I was finally in my suite at the Denver Marriott Hotel City Center. I quickly called Michelle Johnson and told her where I was staying. Michelle took me to all three apartments and I was surprised and pleased by all three. All three were spacious and very lovely with a lot of extras after finding out what the rules and regulations were on them I decided on the second apartment I saw. It was close to shopping centers and to local stores. I also decided that I wanted to also look at luxury homes while I was there maybe buy a nice home if I liked the area enough. A real estate investment for later.

Michelle even called an interior decorator that was a friend of hers to meet us back at the apartment while we waited for Stacy to arrive I signed a six-month lease with the option to renew or to find another place to live. Stacy and I hit it off and decided to meet first thing in the morning to go shopping for furniture.

Michelle took me to the auto dealership to see about I finding my a car. After an hour of test-driving the Mercedes CL600 sports coupe, Lexus RX330 and a Lincoln Navigator I took bought the Mercedes CL600 & the ML350. I drove the CL600 back to the hotel and had the ML350 delivered to the apartment complex first thing in the morning while I was there with Stacy. I made final arrangements with Michelle to get an extra parking stall in the parking garage.

I was still laughing about the look on the dealers face when I told them I would take both cars but one in a white and the other in a silver color. Then I paid for them with my debt card that comes out of my checking account. The look on all of those men's faces when the card purchase was approved was priceless.

Now I was asking the concierge to make arrangements for me to get another limo with the same company as earlier but for service all day to drive Stacy and my around to the different stores. Then I asked him to arrange for a cleaning crew to meet me at the apartment first thing to clean the whole apartment. To get me the phone numbers for the phone company, electric company, cable and anything else he could think of for an apartment. I also asked Ben to get me the number of the best plastic surgeon, and an eye doctor that specialize in laser corrective surgery. The list also included a personal chief and trainer to cook and work in my apartment. Last but not least a day spa that treats women like queens from head to toe. For everything that Ben gets done I will give him a fifty dollar bill. Ben smiled at me and told me he would personally make sure to get it done by the time I return.

I went up to my room and ordered room service. Then put away all of my things and began to pull out my laptop. Even picking out my apartment and getting an interior decorator, I will still have to stay at the hotel for another week or two until the whole apartment is decorated. Eventually I would like to have my dream home built in Denver and Dallas. I will give Michelle Johnson another call tomorrow and see if I could recommend a top architect to design my dream home. It won't hurt to have property in Denver I can make it my summer home if I want to later.

I just began working on my laptop to update my plan when the door knocked I was sure it was room service with my order. I sat down to the table in the room and ate my meal, then quickly got back to updating my plan. I had one small phase complete finding a place to live now I just have to get all moved in. I will not go back to Kansas unless I absolutely had to until my plan is done.

I will make weekly calls to my six best friends and when my plan is done I will invite them out for a girl's weekend spending spree my treat.

Having Ben chase down all of the little things for me will save me a ton of time later so that I can concentrate on the big picture. I thought of one more thing that I needed Ben to chase down for my so I will write it down and give it to him in the morning. By the time that Ben got all of the information that I wanted his bonus was a good fifteen hundred dollars but I gave him two thousand.

Based on the list that Ben gave me, I was able to go with his recommendations, for a chief, personal trainer and spa. Ben had even gotten the phone numbers to all of the things that I would need for the apartment. I first called the personal trainer and he came right over to meet with me. I liked Dan right from the moment I met him, so much so I told him what I wanted to accomplish and Dan told me what he would have me do. I hired Dan right then and there.

"Jasmine I have your workout schedule all planed out. I talked with the bicycle shop that I always go too and told them what you needed and we will bring over several bikes for you to try." "Dan ask for them to bring over a few choices for you as well. "How soon do you want to start your workout?" "Well once I get moved into my apartment which will be in 1 - 2 weeks we can start right away."

"We will start at sunrise we will rotate different workouts for each day this will help keep you focused. Is there any kind of sport or activity that you have wanted to do but have not?"

"Well I like the biking, walking is good, I love watching football but I don't want to play the game." "From what I've learned from you in the past few hours you can have anything you want."

After Dan left I called Mario the chief that Ben had suggested. Mario had asked me a lot of questions and made an appointment to come see me the very next day. Mario told me that he would bring some samples of his work for me to try that would meet my requirements.

The next day Mario came to my hotel room with lots of samples for me to try. I thought that I had died and gone to heaven the food was wonderful. I could hardly believe that it was all healthy, low fat and low in carbs. "Mario this food is so good that I can hardly stop eating it. As soon as I get moved into my apartment I would love for you start." "Well Miss Jasmine I'm all yours just give me a call when you find out when you will move into your apartment. Since you will be getting your apartment setup I will cook your meals in my kitchen and bring them over to you each day."

"Once you're ready for me to cook in your kitchen just let me know. I will tell you that there is a certain brand of pots that I like to cook in." "That's fine Mario just go get what you need and bring me back the receipt." "I will shop for the china that I would like to use. I would also like for you to meet my personal trainer and work with him on my eating plan to accelerate my weight loss." "Miss Jasmine, can I ask you why you want to lose weight? I mean you look wonderful as is." "Thank you Mario, but I have a goal to meet and the only way to do that is to lose weight and to get into shape."

"Mario and I talked and came up with a good eating plan for you including your past and present health conditions. Your meals will be healthy and will include some of your favorite meals."

One week later with the help of Stacy had my apartment 75 percent decorated, and all of the furniture pieces picked out but waiting on delivery of the pieces that had to be ordered even with express delivery it would be another few days before it would all be in for Stacy to arrange them. Stacy had the kitchen, two bathrooms, and the exercise room done. Stacy had half of the living room and dining room furniture in. My bedroom furniture was all on order and will be delivered in the next three days. In the meantime, Stacy and I picked out linens for both bedrooms. Stacy took the lead on all of the accessories based on the colors and furniture selections that I made.

Stacy also talked with a local art gallery and had them bring over some selections for me to look through and decide on.

I called both Mario and Dan on a conference call and told them that all of the furniture was now delivered and that we could begin first thing Monday morning.

"You will drink plenty of water during the day and Mario will have healthy snacks for you in between your workouts". "Dan just don't kill me with this workout, I have a big job to do when the weight is all off."

"I promise when I'm done with my work with you, you will be very pleased." Dan even when I get the weight off your work may not be done, I will need help maintaining and staying in shape. Not to mention when my surgery is complete I will need your help getting back on my feet and to stay in shape."

The very next day the bicycle shop brought over several bikes for me to ride around the parking lot. I picked out my bike after four tries and told Dan to pick him out one as well. When we were done I had wrote out a check to the bike shop for two thousand dollars. I told them to add in the bike helmets, shoes, biking shorts, tops and riding sunglasses.

The bike shop promised to deliver the bikes in two days after making final adjustments. Dan and I started working on my other workout program.

My first day felt like torture but Dan was wonderful and patient with me. Dan kept telling me how wonderful I was doing and that kept my going and trying harder than ever. I knew that Mike would not have said a positive word to me just all negative. By the end of the first two hours I was dripping in sweat, and my muscles were feeling very sore and weak. In fact they felt like a wet noodle and my legs like rubber wobbling all over the place. Dan was giving me a break so I was on my second 32 oz of water in the last hour. "Miss Jasmine what kind of smoothie would you like for after your workout?" "I would love anything with strawberries, bananas, kiwi, passion fruit. Just surprise me Mario."

When I was done with my 1st workout Mario surprised me by telling my how well I was doing, and how fast I will lose the weight. "I have all the faith in the world that you will do it Jasmine." "Thank you Mario that means a lot." "The Thai Chi coach will come by tomorrow. Jasmine do you mind if I call you J?" "I don't mind at all Dan my boss use to call me J." I found myself a little excited about learning Thai Chi. I started to think about how when I was married and the girls were still at home I would not have done this at all. Now I am taking out the time to learn from the best and to try something new. "J are you sure that you want to learn boxing? It is a rough sport." "Let me try it once and see if I like it Dan, I have to try it to know for sure"

Later I was trying to get my new schedule straight in my head. Monday, Wednesday, and Saturday morning Dan and I ride our bikes for two hours. Then we come back and work half an hour with weights in the apartment gym room. On Tuesday, Thursday, will be the Thai Chi, and Core Secrets. Friday is step aerobics.

I walked slowly to my master bath and began the whirlpool tub. Every muscle ached and I could barely move. I took an Aleve and waited for the tub to fill up. Dan had already left and I had told Mario to give my at least 30 minutes in the whirlpool then I would eat my lunch.

I continued to do my workout faithfully every day. After the 1st week, I had lost 3 pounds and Dan measured 2 inches total. I felt wonderful after hearing that both Dan and Mario brought me half dozen roses for my weight loss. Dan and Mario were my biggest fans and support system right now. They had no clue of how important their support was to me. I knew that in the end this would make me happy but with their caring, and support has made me want to make them proud of me and my success.

I thought that the only way at this point to know if changes had worked if a man could look at me and can't take his eyes of me. Now that would be the ultimate feeling if a man follows me like a dog in heat. I smiled to myself thinking that all of the torture and pain would be worth it and only time will tell. I still had a long way to go, I still had to lose 72 pounds and get my body in the best shape ever.

In one of our many talks Dan had asked me what kind of body I wanted. I laughed and had told him that I wanted abs & a body like Janet Jackson, and looks like Halle Berry.

Dan had told me that he could help my get as close to the body of Janet Jackson but he could not help me on the looks of Halle Berry. "J just know that it will not happen overnight and it will be a lot of hard work."

"I know Dan but I can still dream and picture the results." 'Yes you can and I know that you can and will do it, don't believe anyone that says you can't.' "Thanks Dan I really appreciate your support and encouragement. It helps me stay focused."

'J, why do you say that I?" 'Because when I was married my husband ignored me, always had either nothing or negative things to say, never told me that I looked nice or even how proud of me he was. If he did it was so rare that I always felt as though he was saying that to keep me under his thumb. If I had something good happening in my life, like when I finally graduated from college. My husband could not find time to take off work to be home to see me walk with my class. He did not even say he was proud of me for being done with my degree. Or when I joined a sorority he said nothing. When I changed my hairstyle or bought a new dress he said nothing. It was as if I was invisible. I was only good for taking care of him and our daughters. I meant nothing to him. Dan my husband would not talk to me unless he had something to say to me, or wanted me to do something for him. If I tried to talk to him, he always acted as if I was interrupting him or what I had to say didn't matter. When I made suggestions or gave my input on something he treated me as if my ideas were always wrong or stupid. But then I would be right on the money and he would never say you were right I should have listened.

"J your husband was a fool a very big fool. You are more than a woman than he will ever know and any man would be damn lucky to have you by his side."

"Thanks Dan but look at me now, all I ever got from him was a lot of heartache and pain. I've been hurt beyond belief. I found out after he died that he had affairs, so what does that say about me as a wife." "It tells me that he was the stupid one and that he did not appreciate you for who you where/are. Tell me I what do you want to do with your life and career after you reach your goal?"

"That is a good question I have not decided on yet. I think a new career is in order but who knows it all depends on what becomes available. Maybe something in public relations, I love football maybe I can work on a NFL team behind the scenes. Open my own business or just take it easy for a year. Maybe do some charity work with one or two of my favorite charities. It is still too early to tell ask me again in six months or in one year. I want to do something meaningful to make a difference."

"J, if an NFL hires you, you had better look out." "Why is that Dan?"

"Well I think that you're hot now and when you reach your goal you will have men standing in line following you like a dog in heat." I laughed "We shall see Dan we shall see doubtful but who knows anything is possible. Not to mention if that happens I will owe you and Mario a big bonus for getting me there."

The next day Dan and I was hard at work with my workout. When I was done I felt good and not in pain like I was the day before, still a little rubber legs but not bad. Like the day before when I was done with my workout I climbed into my whirlpool tub. The tub helped keep my muscles lose and my knots in my back and neck was losing up but I really needed a massage.

I decided to call the Egyptian spa that Ben told my about. As soon as I was done with my lunch I found the number, called and found out that we were booked solid for the next two days. I asked if any of their massage therapist would be willing to come to my apartment today and get a one hundred dollar tip on top of whatever they would charge me for coming today. Mandy the spa coordinator said that I would check with the therapists and give me a call back in a few minutes. While I had Mandy on the line I asked her what was the next available time they had open for a full day of pampering. Mandy said she would look at the schedule and call me back in a few minutes.

My phone did ring 10 minutes later "Jasmine this is Mandy Jessie will be at your apartment around 6:30 this evening if that will be ok with you. The next available day for a full day of pampering would be Thursday at 10:00. "Yes, Mandy I looked forward to meeting Jessie at 6:30 and the 10:00 Thursday would be perfect too. I'm new to the Denver area can you please give me the directions to get to the salon." I give Mandy my address to give to Jessie. I wanted to wait until I met Jessie before making a standing appointment for the massage.

At 6:30 that evening, Jessie showed up at my door. Since I had massages at spas before I was already undressed and in my robe. I let Jessie in and told her that she could setup her table in the living room. Dan and Mario had already left for the day, so I did not have to worry about my privacy. Jessie asked me a few questions to know what my trouble spots are. Then Jessie turned down all of the lights and put a cd in my player. Jessie worked on me for an hour and a half. I was so relaxed that I had fallen asleep sometime during the massage. Jessie had to wake me when the time was up.

"Jessie would you be able to do this every week maybe three times I would make it worth your while? You will get a weekly tip on top of what I give for an hour massage, if you would consider being on my payroll in addition to your regular job?" "Jasmine thank you I would really like to do that. I really needed the work and the extra money." "Great Jessie I also look forward to come to the spa I really can't way to splurge." Jessie then informed me that the "current owner is wanting to sell the business since the original owner died of a heart attack and the new owners were really not wanting to remain in the business and is looking to sell."

I did not say anything to Jessie but decided to wait until I saw for myself before I decided if I would be interested in buying the spa. I had called Mandy the next day and asked if it would be ok if I would arrive around 9:30 to take a tour of the spa and ask a few questions. Mandy told I that would be fine.

When I arrived on Thursday morning I did not have to wait long I fell in love with the spa the moment I walked in. Mandy was waiting at the door for me since the spa normal hours are at 10:00. "Jasmine would you like anything to drink?" "A glass of water would be great." Mandy got my water and then we walked around the business. I was impressed with what I saw. There was not much that I would want to change as far as decorations it was set up just about the way I would want it to be. I asked Mandy how busy are they on a weekly basis and what's the yearly business expenses and gross? Mandy gave the overview of the numbers and the name of the owners lawyers if I was interested in more detailed information about the business and what the yearly numbers are. Mandy also told me that the spa has only been open for two years.

By the time that we were done with the tour it was time for my day of pampering to begin. We first started with a facial that took an hour and a half then my lunch was ready. Mandy came into the room and asked me if I would like to help test out a new machine that is being demonstrated to the shop today. Mandy wanted to get a customer's opinion of if the machine before committing to the purchase or leasing of one or two. Or at least put it on a list to budget for it later in the year.

I was impressed with the aqua massage table. "Mandy how many people did they have on the payroll?" "Well we have 4 hair stylists, 2 nail technicians, 4 massage therapists, 3 facial technicians, 1 full-time & 2 part-time receptionist."

For the next few weeks I worked in my weekly spa treatments and said nothing about my growing desire to buy the spa. I got in touch with the lawyer of the new owners and asked what was the asking price of the spa. The lawyer told me that we were asking for four hundred thousand dollars. I talked with Mr. Stokes and asked him to review the contract and to make a counter offer with just a few changes with an offer of three hundred and fifty thousand.

Working Hard

I STARTED TO NOTICE AFTER MY first month of working out and eating right that the weight was starting to melt off. I noticed that my size 16/18 pants were too big. The next day Dan and I took my measurements and weight. I jumped up and down for joy when I saw I had lost 15 pounds and 5 inches in my first month. I was so excited I gave Dan and Mario a bonus in their next paycheck. Dan decided that we would only weigh and measure every month so the following month I had lost to my amazement another 12 pounds and 3 inches. "If you keep this up the wind will blow you away." "Dan you have no idea how long I've wanted to lose this weight and what I've tried to get it off. Now I'm seeing results I'm going to have to buy some new clothes again, last month I was in a 14 now I think I can get into a 12 or maybe a 10. "Jasmine you said that you wanted to get into a size 6 well you're on your way you should be able to do that in the next oh 2 months maybe if we keep this workout going." "Good then the next phase will begin." "What phase is that J?" "Well I plan on seeing a plastic surgeon to get rid of any access skin that the exercise doesn't and some other things that I feel needs to be worked on." "Wow J you're looking wonderful now you don't need any surgery if you don't mind me saying so." "Thanks Dan but your biased you're working on improving my body with exercise and its working now when we are done with the major stuff the minor things will be ready to happen. Remember I will still need your help when it's all done to get back into shape and remain there."

"J don't worry I will be here for you whenever you need me. Not to mention I want to see what you plan on doing." Dan and I had a good laugh. "I'm not telling you will just have to wait and see."

The third month I only lost 10 pounds which put my at a total of 37 pounds lost so far. "Look Jasmine don't get discouraged you have done very well losing this much in only 3 months not to mention the inches you've lost so far." "I know but this is the least amount of weight I've lost so far, I don't understand why we haven't changed anything." "I think that your body is getting use to the routine that we created we will just have to up the routine and amount of time to your workout." "You mean that I will have to work out even longer then I do now?" "Yes you will if you want the weight to come off. Let's start by another half hour and see if that helps I will weigh and measure you once a week and see if that will make a difference if not then we will change up the program." "Well damn Dan can we just change the program around try something different now?" "J are you sure you want to change?" "Not really but lets try it the only thing I have to lose is weight."

"Dan your going to kill me before this is all over." "Thanks I think that when you're all done then you will love me." "You may be right, just be careful, I don't think that you will be able to handle me when I'm all done."

In the fourth month I had increased my 2 hour work outs to 2 /12 - 3 throughout the day, and Dan changed and rotated my work out. I saw even more of a difference with changing the routine adding more did wonders. I found I was more limber, my abs was starting to get a small six-pack outline but not like Janet Jackson's yet but I was determined to get there. Then I noticed that my but was getting smaller and rounded again. I noticed that I had not lost anything in my breasts so without a doubt I would have them lifted and maybe reduced a little when the time comes. At the end of month 4 I weighed and Dan told me the increase made a difference I was now done another 15 pounds and I only had another 23 pounds to lose. I was very hopeful that I could loose it all in the next 2 months. I had to laugh I was now into a size 8 I haven't been this size for years. I was getting smaller and all most back to a size 6 just one more dress size and I will be there.

The next month I weighed in was now only 4 pounds away to my goal weight. I also saw that I lost even more inches and now I had by-passed my goal size. I was now in a size 4 I couldn't believe it a size 4 I never thought I would get down to that size ever I was happy to be a size 6 again but a size 4 was a dream. "So J what size are you into now?" "Dan you won't believe it I'm in a size 4 a 4 I never thought I would ever be this small." "Well you are now only 4 pounds from your goal weight do you still want to keep going?" "No I think I'm happy here just need to maintain." "Ok then set up a new training schedule and eating plan. We will work out every day but only for 1 hour. I will also talk to Mario and have him work up a new calorie count for you."

"J are you ready to get weighed and measured?" "Yes, Dan I'm ready let me have the news." "Well I you now weigh 104 and your measurements are to die for, your now 38-22-24. J, you have worked so hard and you look amazing."

"Oh Dan, you and Mario you are absolutely wonderful. You have earned a wonderful bonus for helping me make and surpass my goals. Not only that what are you doing tonight, let's go out to celebrate my treat you both earned it." "You're on Jasmine we will be back here at what 6:30 is that ok or do you want later?" "Let's make it 7 I will let you two pick the place make the reservations. I will order a car for us."

After Dan and Mario left I decided to go shopping and made a quick call to the spa to get my hair done. I bought all new clothes to match my new figure. I was in shock and delight to find out I was now in a size 2 and I vowed to stay that size with the help of Dan and Mario. That night I took, Dan, and Mario out to celebrate my weight loss.

"Ok so when will the big day be?" "Are you talking about the surgery? Well that will be once I meet with a doctor I'm comfortable with and see what can be done. Even though I've lost all my weight and I'm now in a size 2 I have excess skin that did not go away even with all of the exercising Dan made me do. I think I'm going to do a tummy tuck, but & breast lift and something with my arms."

"Wow Jasmine, are you sure you want to go through that drastic surgery?" "Well Mario I might be able to do something else other than a tummy tuck maybe liposuction but I will need to fix my nose. I won't know for sure until I see a dr. Look, both of you have worked really hard with me and I need you both to continue to work with me to keep me like this and better. We will still have lots of work to do even after the surgery. I will request a nurse while I'm recovering my first few weeks home. I will still need you to cook for me Mario and for a modified workout while I heal Dan. Not to mention your now part of my family. So you two might as well get use to the idea and I want you both to know that I will be working on a project. I will be following through with another goal that I want to work on but had to lose the weight first. You may see or hear things that may shock you that I will have to do. I have to have my day of revenge." (No you really don't my daughter I will take care of them if you let me) Lord I'm sorry I am truly sorry but I can't do that right now. (Let Go Jasmine and let me handle it for you) I will starting tomorrow right after I investigate these 4 doctors that are well known for their work.

Your All Woman

Wow I can't believe the change in my body. I was amazed looking at my naked body. I was staring at my body in the full-length mirror seeing the difference the exercise had made. I just can't believe it, I won't have to have too much surgery done. Maybe cool sculpting on my stomach instead of a full tummy tuck. Cool sculpting for thighs, hips, and a breast reduction. Other than that I have to admit that I looked good and felt very sexy. Now it was time to put it to the test and see if men found my just as sexy.

I found myself extremely horny for the first time in a long time. I wanted to be in the arms of a man even if it was just for one night. I hate one night stands but I found myself wanting a man to touch me and treat me as if we could not do without me. I felt like a tigress on the prowl for my prey.

I figured I had enough time to go shopping for some new sexy clothes and a few books. I knew that there are plenty of things that I'm ignorant about sexually. All my life I had been told that good girls don't talk about sex, good girls don't do anything but the missionary position. Well

I decided it was time to be a little bad and I would start at the book store to educate myself. "OMG" you can do that tilting my head, oh my no way no way…

Ok no one ever said anything about, and Mike and I never tried that or this. Even before Mike I never thought or did Oh My, oh holy crap. I quickly closed the book picked up the others I had put on the floor that I planned to buy and quickly went up to the cash register to pay. I got my books and left the store with my face red.

Ok talk about eye opening and major shock at the book store but I'm determined to learn all I can. I will learn more than what is just a standard. I will do more than just vanilla.

You're Looking Great

"JASMINE WHEN YOU FIRST CAME to me 3 months ago you had a lot of things that you wanted me to do for you. Now you are better than ever Jasmine. If I weren't your doctor I would ask you out."

"What if I fired you right now would you ask me out doctor, would you even make love to me tonight?"

"Jasmine, I won't lie to you I'm very attracted to you but I don't want just a 1-night stand I want more. Could you handle that?" "Doctor are you sure you want more, I don't want to play any games with you?" "Jasmine I'm sure, I thought that you were beautiful before you came to see me but now you are to die for I want you right now. You're my last appointment for the day let me take you to dinner and we will see where it will take us." "Doctor." "Call me Jason." "Ok Jason I will go to dinner with you and we will see what happens." "Jasmine I can't help myself I have to kiss you." Oh my God, I can't believe that he wants to kiss me, take a deep breath and tell him. "What are you waiting for kiss me Jason" Jason came closer and took my face in his hands and leaned down to kiss me.

"Jason. We better stop now before we can't." "I know your right but I can't stop kissing you right now. I want you right now. I know what your body looks like but I want to see you without your clothes on again. Let me see you again I, let me touch your body not as your doctor but as your lover." "Jason, you have my address to my apartment come over at 6:00 tonight, bring dinner with you. I will be waiting so don't be late."

"Jasmine what do you want to eat?" "Surprise me Jason I will eat anything but I don't think that we will have our minds on eating food right away." "Do you know what you are doing to me?" I think that I know Jason the same thing that you're doing to me." I took Jason's hand and slipped it between my legs. Jason realized that I was hot and wet it took all of his strength not to take my right then and there.

"You better go home and get ready. I will be there before 6:00 and be prepared to stay up late." "Jason, you better tell your receptionist and nurse that you will be in late tomorrow. I don't think that you will be in on time." "You better get out of here now before we end up on the couch, or my desk. I will see you in a few hours."

I have to find something special to wear tonight and I only have a short time to find it." I decided to start with Victoria Secrets and then work my way down to another store.

I looked in the mirror one last time makeup was perfect the slip dress was beautiful, my hair in place the last touch perfume. This would be the first time I would be with a man since my husband died one and a half years ago. I was getting nervous and excided about what would happen tonight. I selected several cd's to put in the changer.

I checked on the wine and started the fireplace. Jason knocked on the door; I took a deep breath and went to the door. Jason stood there in leather jeans, a dress shirt, a dozen white roses, and a bag of food. "Jason please come in." "Wow you look wonderful, the gold dress you have on against your brown hair and eyes wow. What can I say you are so beautiful!" "Thank you Jason are you going to come in or just stand there staring at me?"

"To be totally honest if I come in right now I'm going to make a fool of myself." "Jason it's been so long that I've been with a man that I'm afraid of making a fool of myself." "Let's just take it one step at a time and give this a try." "I hope that those roses are for me?" "Yes they are and I even brought Thai food." "MMMMMMMMM! My favorite, how did you know?"

"I remember you once saying to my nurse that you were on your way to get Thai food. Jasmine your apartment is wonderful. Did you do all of this for tonight? The candles and fireplace is perfect and the music is entrancing." "Jason I hope that you don't mind sitting on the floor by the fireplace?" "I think that would be a wonderful place to start eating dinner." "Jas your right it will be wonderful, lets get dinner setup."

Jason and I went over in front of the fireplace sat down on the pillows I set out earlier in front of the coffee table. I arranged the food onto plates while Jason poured glasses of wine for us. "Jasmine I have controlled myself so far but I'm not sure how much longer I can keep my control." "Jason you don't have to control your self any longer. I want you to kiss me right now." Jason leaned into me and began to kiss me our kiss intensified Jason tore his mouth away and began to trail kisses down my neck and began removing the spaghetti strap from my right shoulder. Oh my God Jason does not know what he is doing. It's been so long and he is making me feel so wonderful, I'm so hot and wet that I'm going to melt and go crazy if Jason doesn't make love to me soon.

"Jason you're making me crazy I'm on fire." "Jasmine I'm already crazy I'm mad for you, I have to have you right now." "Jason take me I'm yours. I began to unbutton Jason's shirt running my hands all over his chest and back. Both Jason and I were looking into each others eyes our hands moving very quickly both not thinking just acting on our impulses and desires. Before either one knew it our clothes were laying on the floor we began to caress each other kissing each others body from head to toe. Jason moved over my body he went down lower over my body sending waves through me.

Jason opened my legs and barred his head between them running his lips over my clit, rubbing it all around with his tongue, sucking my juices. Oh God I'm going to die soon if he doesn't get inside of me. I'm so wet and my juices are so hot, each time I climaxes my juices run like hot water from the faucet, what did the book call it oh yes squirting. "Jason please your making me crazy I want you right now please."

Jason couldn't wait any longer his shaft was in agony Jason leaned back over my body and positioned himself to enter me. Jason tried his best to go slowly at first but I wouldn't let him we were both so hot for each other that our lovemaking was so intense that we both climaxed together. We both lay there in each others arms catching our breath by the fireplace.

"Jasmine I can't believe how wonderful you feel in my arms. I haven't felt like this about any woman or even any client. Even knowing my reasoning for all of the work and pain done in the last 6 months he cared about my deeply. It was more then a physical need it was something more, but he could not understand or explain how.

I laid in Jason's arms thinking how special Jason had become to me in a short amount of time. He told me I was beautiful before when I first came into his office but now I was even hotter. Jason is a special man and I never would have thought that I would ever feel special again by any man.

I decided to give Jason some pleasure and to see if I could help drive him as crazy as he drove me. I went down between his legs and started to lick his shaft. Jason gasp from the pleasure I was causing. "I'm going to explode soon if you keep this up. Jas if you don't stop your magic on me I will explode soon. Oh if you stop, don't stop keep going Jas your tongue and hands are making me crazy. Ok if you stop now I will do any thing you want, Jas please." "Ok Jason make love to me doggie style and then we will try a Kamasutra position."

"Jasmine are you sure this is what you want?" "Jason I want us to do anything and everything we can. Just make love to me lets just make love lets not worry about how or what lets just go with what our instincts take us."

Jason and I continued on for another hour before then stopped and thought about eating some cheese and wine. "Jas tonight has been wonderful I don't want it to end." "It doesn't have too Jason we have all night to spend with each other and enjoy each other's company. Not to mention you did say that you don't want a one-night stand so if that is true tonight is not the only night that we will spend together. Right?" "Yes, that is correct I want you more then just tonight. But I also don't want there to be just sex for us. I want us to really get to know each other."

"Jasmine I'm going to make love to you again but this time I'm going to make love to you in your bed, then in the shower and then back again on the floor." "What are you waiting for?"

I can't believe how Jason made me feel last night and this morning before he left. The love making was out of this world good. I hadn't felt this light hearted and wanted by a man in well in a very long time. (Open your heart my daughter let love fill you from the inside out). Lord what is happening to me I shouldn't be feeling these feelings for Jason this quickly. (My Love doesn't have a time table)

The Girl's Weekend

TAMMY, AMY, LYNNE, MARSHA, KATHY and Diane were all at the airport per the instructions that was in the special delivered notes they all received the week before. Diane and Tammy both received extra special packages as well. They received a Gucci overnight bags and purses. All six ladies had been picked up in a limo that took them to the private airplane waiting for the ladies to fly them to Denver for the weekend.

I made special arrangements for my best friends, the private plane with crew will bring them and a limo will pick them up at the airport and I will be in the limo waiting on them. I decided to give each one three thousand dollars to spend on anything that they wanted for the weekend not to mention that I would buy anything they wanted for the weekend as well.

I was excited to see what my friends thought of my new looks. My hair is longer past my shoulders and my hair color is now a light honey brown. Not to mention that I'm a size six and 110 pounds. All of the procedures that I had are well worth it, I wanted to see if they thought the same.

I saw my friends get off the plane and sunk back into the seat where they couldn't see me until they were all inside. The limo driver was Tommy my favorite limo driver that I asked for often when I needed car service was out of the car opening the door for the ladies as they came closer. They all got in and then notice the extra person in the limo and began to scream with happiness.

At first they were not sure who was in the limo. Then I spoke and all the ladies went wild. "Oh my God, Jasmine where the hell have you been?"

"Jasmine is that really you?" "Jasmine you look gorgeous." "Ok ladies yes it's me, I've been here in Denver the whole time. Do you like the changes I've made?" "What did you do?" "Let's see I've lost 75 pounds, had the ridge in my nose fixed, a little cool sculpting done in a few areas then I grew my hair out and changed the color. Well what do you think?"

"I don't know about everyone else but you look wonderful. I barely recognized you sitting there. Girl you're going to have the men going wild over you." "Diane is right you look good girl you are hot. I love your changes they're great you look beautiful."

"Great I'm glad you all like it now are you ready for this weekend?" "Yes so what are we going to do?" "Well first I've rented out a house that has 7 bedrooms and baths for the whole weekend. We will have the car service at our beck and call all weekend too. I have us all scheduled for a whole day of pampering at a day spa. We will have the whole place to ourselves. Right now we are going shopping and anything you find that you like is on me the whole weekend. And each one of you takes the envelope that has your name on it.

"Before we go any further Jasmine how in the world can you afford all of this?" "Well Amy if I tell you do all of you promise not to tell anyone else?" All of the ladies promised. "Well several months ago I won 20 million dollars in the lottery. Now I'm treating you to a wonderful girl's weekend. You have all been there for me when I needed you the most and I just wanted to do something special for you.

Now you can pull your chins off the floor and lets go have some fun. Tommy!" "Yes Ms. Moore." "Would you please take us to our next destination please." "Yes Ms. Moore."

The ladies all began to laugh and talk, once the limo came to the shopping center we all got out, I told Tommy that I would call him, but Tommy suggested that he walk along with us and he would hold all of their packages and even take them back to the limo while we shopped. All of the ladies loved that idea and began to shop till we all wanted to drop.

I was in constant contact with Mario my chief for the last few hours. He was getting our dinner ready for us and would be ready by the time we got to the house in another hour.

I told the ladies that dinner would be ready in an hour so we had only 30 minutes left before we had to leave to get back to the house. Everyone was ready to eat so that sounded good to them.

I found a nice gift for Jason that I picked up and everyone wanted to know who it was for. I just smiled and began telling my friends about Jason. All of their mouths fell to the floor again. 'I can't believe you, you hussy." I didn't take offence by my friend's words; I knew that they didn't mean for it to be an insult. "Well after dinner I will tell you all the rest of the story and you won't say that." Lynne replied "this should be good." "I think we will need drinks for this story, Jasmine and you better not leave anything out is all I have to say! I want to hear all the dirty details." "Good grief, we will have champagne tonight and any other drinks you desire. We will also be waited on hand and foot with a butler, maid, chief and limo driver all weekend."

"Jasmine we can't thank you enough for this wonderful treat, but I still can't believe you didn't tell us you won the lottery before now." "I just want you all to be relaxed, happy, and enjoy this weekend. Now let's sit back and enjoy being coffered around in a limo. Mario is the chief he has been fixing all of my meals for the last several months. This has helped me greatly, and then sometime tomorrow I will take you by the apartment so you can see what I've done with it and the house that I'm thinking about buying here." "Is this because of that handsome Dr. Jason of yours?" "Maybe only time will tell but I love the area who knows I may decide to move to Seattle or Dallas instead. It's too early to tell right now."

We pulled into the driveway of a mansion that Michelle Johnson helped I arranged for the weekend with the option to think about buying the house. I was in the house earlier and not sure if I wanted to commit to this house just yet. I introduced the ladies to the hired help for the weekend and to Mario the chief. The butler and maid assisted Tommy with getting all of the luggage and shopping bags out of the limo, sorted and placed in each room correctly.

In the mean time Mario had brought his assistant with him to take care of the ladies and their meal needs. All of the ladies went to their rooms first and then came straight down for dinner Mario had different cheeses and appetizers out. But all of the ladies wanted the real food. Mario had out done himself with a lamb dinner and salads. Then the door bell rang just as the ladies were all getting up to go sit by the fireplace to talk and have dessert.

The butler introduced Jason and all of the ladies sat straight up eyes all glued to the door. I watched as their mouths fell to the floor for the 3rd or 4th time today. I got up to meet Jason and to get a kiss. Jason had 2 dozen roses for me and a rose each for all of my friends. All of the girls fell in love with Jason at that moment.

Jason then shocked us all and said "I just wanted all of you to know and to tell Jasmine that I'm madly in love with her and I wanted to make her happy for the rest of her life." "Jasmine, I know we haven't known each other long but I feel in love with you the moment I met you." Now it was my turn to have my mouth fall to the floor. Jason knew that men had hurt me very badly in my past and he wanted to be the one that to make the pain go away and help me live again.

Jason knew that I would never agree to marry him until I was done with my plans for revenge if he could not change my mind. But he was willing to stay and keep trying to win my love and heart. (Let go of the revenge my daughter it is not what you need. What you need is love, love me first, then love yourself and then love others. Jason can help you heal your heart he is what you need at this moment.)

I was still in shock at Jason's announcement to my best friends. If Jason only knew just how much in love I am with him that would set him over the edge. I was not ready to tell him how much I loved him because of all the men in my past that hurt me to my core. Not to mention that I had vowed to myself that I would not fall in love again. Somewhere along the lines Jason worked his magic and I fell in love with him.

Jason finished talking and eating dessert with the ladies and said goodnight. I walked Jason to his car to say goodnight. Jason pulled me into his arms leaning against his Jaguar kissing me. Jason then pulled his lips away. "Jasmine I was serious earlier when I told all of your friends that I'm in love with you. I am truly in love with you but I know you have something you have to do that you will end soon. I hope that you will one day be able to tell me that you love me as well."

"Yes Jason I know and once my plan is done then I will have my new life and we can talk about us then ok. I promise Jason this will all be over soon and then we can talk about us." "I will hold you to that you realize that don't you?" "Yes Jason I do realize it and know you will."

"Good then kiss me one more time and I will leave as hard as it will be. I will be very lonely this weekend without you." "Jason if you don't get out of here now I will sneak you into my room." "Jas you drive me wild." "Yes Jason just as wild as you drive me so turnaround is fair play."

Jason finally pulled himself away from me so that I could spend time with all of my friends. Jason did consider coming back later in the night and sneaking into Jasmine's room. If he did that we would make way to much noise making love and all of my friends would know. But maybe just maybe they could be quiet....Jason drove around to the back of the house and let himself in.

I went back into the house as Jason pulled away and all of my friends where standing at the door waiting on me. They all started in with questions and comments about how good Jason looked and wanted to know how old he was, if he had a single brother or single friends, and if he could do surgery on them for free. I barely kept up with all of the questions they threw at me but I was finally able to answer all of their questions laughing.

I decided to tell my friends about Mike and what I learned. There was a long discussion about how I knew deep down from somewhere that I did not want to face before how Mike was a flat out no doubt about it a DOG. "Ok I also want to tell you that I've been planning revenge on all the ladies that Mike had an affair with and all of the men that hurt me deeply in my past." "Jasmine are you sure you want to do that?" "Diane what do you suggest that I do instead? How can I let go of dishing out revenge?" "The best revenge my friend/my sister is to let go and let God take care of it. They will be dealt something far worse by God it's called Karma."

"Jasmine, give your anger, hurt emotions over to God to heal your heart. Turn lose all of the negative energy. It won't do you a damn bit of good holding onto it."

"Jaz are you sure that this won't come back later karma wise to cause you more harm and pain?" "I don't think so but who really knows for sure." "I can't believe what I'm hearing Jasmine I can't believe you would do or even think of something like this you of all people." "What are you talking about Tammy?" "I could see me doing something like this to plan revenge but you no way not in a million years. You always said you treated people by the 'Golden Rule'. I don't believe you are considering this it is not like you. I know Mike hurt you and the other men but no way not you." "I agree with Tammy I can't believe you of all people Jasmine." "Ok Tammy & Lynne I hear you and when you put it that way yes it sounds really bad, and I can't believe I'm saying this. It really doesn't feel like me either but I was just so mad and wanted to lash out at something or someone. I was tired of having people step all over me." "Jasmine they won't step all over you unless you let them. I think you are a strong woman and a woman of color no less. Look at all of the things you've accomplished in your life. That speaks volumes and you getting past all of the hurt and lies say even more about you."

I couldn't help it the tears started. "Oh Jazzy let it all out but I agree with Tammy, Diane and Lynne, you don't have to use revenge to feel better." Come here group hug time let it all out Jasmine we are your sisters we are always here for you. Besides you got that hot doctor at your beck and call and he just said bravely in front of all of us that he loves you and that is more important than any revenge ever could be." "Damn Amy you preach sister." "Kathy shut up and get over here to join the hug. You know I'm right. Hell if Jasmine doesn't get that doctor Jason of her's to propose can I have him?" "Marsha" all the ladies said at the same time. "What I'm just saying damn he's fine, I wouldn't mind a piece of." "Marsha" Diane said. "Ok, ok sorry Jas you know I wouldn't take your man but really does he have a brother?" "Marsha" I said giggling. "Now that is the Jasmine that I know and love."

Just then Jasmine heard and saw the light go off in her head. "Girls thank you are all right. That is what I needed to hear all of you say. That is what God has been trying to tell me but I was just too focused on dishing out my own form of justice and revenge." As Jasmine stood there in her friends arms she prayed. God I'm sorry please forgive me for wanting revenge it's not mine to do. I turn it all over to you. I want love in my life I choose Jason to give my love to and to receive love from.

It was 1:00 am before we all decided to go to bed and get a few hours before we have breakfast at 7:30 and their day of pampering to start at 8:30. We all talked about what we would wear tomorrow and I told them that it would not matter because we may all be in bath robes until we are ready to do our hair and makeup last.

I knew that my friends would enjoy their day of pampering to take place tomorrow. Little did I know that Jason also planned a night of pampering for me. Jason had made arrangements champagne and a fruit tray waiting in my room and lit candles everywhere. He was hoping that I would not be staying up talking with my friends. Jason was standing in the shadows between the bedroom and the bathroom door as I entered the room. I stopped dead in my tracks as I closed the door. Jason stepped out holding a glass of champagne for me. "I couldn't leave you Jasmine, you are the woman that I've always dreamed of. I can't live life without you I know you have something important to do but I thought I could wait but I can't." Jason stepped back a step reached into his pocket and got down on one knew. "Jasmine will you do me the honor and become my wife, marry me Jas, let me love you forever?"

I blinked once, twice but couldn't see Jason from the tears streaming down my face. "Jason, before I answer you I have to tell you. I love you. I've been in love with you for months. Yes, yes I will marry you." Jason stood up taking my hand and slipping the ring on to it. O M G I looked down to find a 3 carat emerald cut halo engagement ring on my finger. "Jason it's beautiful" "Jas do you really like it? If you don't we can go pick out something else." I cut Jason off by kissing him. Kissing Jason always makes me want to curl my toes.

Since I started seeing Jason I made it a mission to find beautiful nightgowns and lingerie to wear one Jason loves when I do and it makes my feel good. Thank God I put on set of sexy bra and matching panties. Jason won't be going home tonight. Jason began to run his hand up the inside of my leg to my very center of my body. Jason knew that his touch causes my body to respond and I become hot almost instantly. I'm not exactly sure when or how for that matter our clothes came off and the comforter was on the floor along with the pillows. Jason was thrusting inside of me before I knew it.

We laid there for a minute after our first fast and furious section panting trying to catch our breath. "Damn Jason I would have told you I loved you before now if I knew you would react like this." I said giggling. "Baby you haven't seen anything yet roll over onto your stomach. Let me love you from behind." As we slowed the pace down Jason had me coming two more times but he held back. "Jasmine I'm not going to cum for you yet. I'm not done with you I want you to be so pleasured you will scream my name before this night is out.

Jason wasn't kidding about pleasuring me all night. Jason did have me screaming his name before morning came. I just hope that the girls didn't hear us. He finally came after I called out his name. We laid there in each other's arms until the alarm went off. I felt so lucky and so loved after all of the pain. I finally let go of all the fear of being in love and happy.

Jason was not letting me out of the bed until we made love again. I climaxed two more times before Jason had his climax. "You were so beautiful lying on the floor this morning in my arms. Jasmine the next time we make love I will make you squirt. Do you know what that is?" I shook my head no. "What is that I've never heard that term before?" "That is the ultimate orgasm a woman can have." I will help you get there Jas believe me." "Damn

Jason if what you did to me last night didn't get me there after how many orgasms then what in the world." "Just wait love you will see"

"Ok Jason, will you please come back again tonight?" "Oh I will be in your room by 10:00 do you think that you can get away from your friends?" "I will find away, hell who knows I may just say hey Jason is here and we will be taking care of business tonight. That should get some laughs out of them."

I finally made it downstairs for breakfast with the ladies before leaving for the spa. I knew by the look on my friends faces they knew what happened last night or this morning. "So Jasmine how did you sleep last night? Did you have any nightmares?" "No nightmares, I slept great and you?" "Wow I'm shocked you said that with a straight face you hussy." "What in the world are you talking about Tammy?" "Jasmine let me tell you what I'm talking about pretending that you were going to bed last night and you had a man in your room. In fact Jason came back didn't he?" "What makes you say that?" "What makes you say that? She asks well lets see ladies correct me if I'm wrong but didn't you hear like I did Jasmine screaming out Jason's name once last night and once this morning or a bed banging against the wall and a man yelling out Jasmine's name?"

Oh boy they did hear everything as my face turned beat red as I hid held my head down looking at my coffee mug. "Well ladies I'm sorry, yes Jason surprised me last night or I should say when we all went to bed this morning. He was waiting in my room with candles, roses, champagne. Then he got down on his knee and asked me to marry him so you tell me what would you have done?" I looked up at my best friends to see all of their mouths hanging open. "He did WHAT" "He asked me to marry him and I said Yes." As I put out my left hand and wiggled my fingers. The ladies all jumped up and grabbed my hand. "Damn Jas, Congratulations, Girl when are you marrying him…" "That Jason has good taste in rings and in women. Look at you all glowing and stuff." "We're happy for you Jasmine you deserve to be happy and to have someone love you like Jason." "So are you going to tell us what all happened?"

Diane yelled "that is none of our business unless Jasmine wants to share then that is another story." Right I? "Yes Diane your right." "Well!"

"Well what Jasmine? Are you going to tell us or not, inquiring minds want to know?" "Ok I will say is this it was wow all night long. There are you satisfied?" "NO, Jasmine, you will have to do better than that, I mean really!" "Jasmine they won't shut up until you give them some details." Diane said. I started laughing at my dear friends. "Are you sure uour ears aren't too young for graphic details? Let me say I'm sorry now girls if you don't get much sleep before going home tomorrow."

"Come on Jasmine I/we need some new ideas to try on our men when we get home." "Alright the pace and the positions were all based and set by Jason to give me pleasure. Ok try the Deep Union from the Kamasutra." "The what, from what?" "The deep union from the kamasurta." I explained the position. The woman has to be kneeling with her back to her lover, the female is incapable of moving. The man covers the woman's loins with one hand and with the palm of the other massages the woman's but." "Oh my goodness Jasmine do you two do kinky stuff." "No not kinky we just like to try different things to give us pleasure." "Oh come on ladies you can't tell me that you all are old maid's and only do the missionary position, or what do they call it now vanilla?"

"Ok we are all going shopping at an Adult store to see if they have the book?" "Jasmine we can't go into that kind of store." "Don't tell me that you're all prudes and close minded? We can and we will go to an adult store. I lost the fight with my friends to go to the adult store so I asked Tommy the limo driver to first call around to the stores to see if any of them carry the book and if they had six copies. Tommy found a store and came back with six copies for us.

Diane and Kathy let their copies sit there while they stared at them. "Ok you two it's just a book with information in it. It's not porn look at it as finding new exciting ways to make love to your man. Just look at the pictures so that you see the actual position. It's not dirty, just look at the book."

"Jasmine you are too wild and crazy, I will look if Kathy does." "Diane you're crazy just like Jasmine but we will look at it together ok." "Ok."

"Jasmine what did Jason do to you to make you say what you said last night?" I looked at Amy with a puzzled look on my face. "Amy what did I say last night?" "Jasmine you don't remember?" Amy Jason was in the room we said a lot of things the whole night. I really have no idea of what I said out loud or was screaming in my head."

Amy started laughing. "Jas you said and I quote. Dear Mary mother of Jesus in heaven! And then it was quiet except for the couple of squeaks from your bed. Then I heard a couple of moans and then nothing." I smiled replaying last night in my head. I had to shake myself out of my dream state. To be honest he rocked my world more than one. I think I said that when he went down on me or it could have been when we made love doggie style or it could have been one of the 3 Kamasutra positions we did."

Amy and the others started laughing along with me. We finish up our breakfast and all got into the limo to go over to the spa. My friends saw the name of the spa once we got out and they all looked at me and said that the name 'The Egyptian Spa' sounded like something that I would pick out. I laughed and said yes it is.

I went into the spa and talked with the spa manager Mandy. Mandy welcomed everyone and offered them all a mimosa to drink. Drinks in hand everyone was taken back to the dressing rooms with little lockers. The spa is a full line of services to pamper the customer. Every guest is offered a terry robe for all their serves to put on while the person is being pampered. I had fallen in love with the spa the first time I came.

Little did my friends know that I had bought the spa 3 months ago. I could not resist buying the business. I felt that I got a wonderful deal out of it and the profits keep rising enough that I could open a second spa across town. The decorations and feel to the place was out of this world, it made me think that I was in Greece with a touch of Egypt. I have an office in the spa for when I do come in or want to work. I just finished redecorating the office to give it my style and comfort.

I talk with Mandy every week about the spa and any problems that may or may not happen. I had a really good mentor/teacher with my old boss before I quit working. I still talk with him every two weeks. Now I get to use what I learned from him on a daily bases and a little from college with my business. I even get a few new ideas for the spa talking with Adam on regular bases. I even sent him 2 first class tickets for him and his wife to come to Denver and told him that they could have a full day of pampering on me.

I'm seriously thinking about expanding and have another business if I do that I will have to create a corporation.

I wonder if I can get Adam to work for me as one of my executives.

Right now the ladies and I all were getting different services done all at the same time. A few of us were together getting manicures and pedicures. 2 were getting massages and 2 were getting facials. Around lunch time we were back into a center relaxation room. Mandy took us back to a recently remodeled room that we turned into a small dining room. Once lunch was over we had another hour of spa services. Then we were off to go shopping.

We were all like little kids at Christmas, laughing, giggling, acting silly enjoying ourselves shopping. Some of the ladies had to buy another piece of luggage to take everything home with them tomorrow. I spent another ten thousand dollars on my friends and I felt that it was well worth it. Not to mention that I spent another four thousand on myself.

I realized I hadn't had this much fun or this relaxed with my friends in a long time. I wanted to do this kind of thing more often. "Ladies I have to ask you if I send you notes saying pack your bags for you and your spouse go to the airport and be prepared to fly would you come no questions asked?"

"Yes Jasmine if the note came from you I would." "If this weekend is any indication of the fun we had yes I would too no questions asked." "Diane what about you?" "Yes you're my little sis yes I would come and you know I don't like to fly." Amy stepped up to me. "I will come or go anywhere you would ask me. You call we will come."

"Ok good just know that we will do this again. This will be a time to enjoy and remember."

The Difference

T HE DIFFERENCE BETWEEN MIKE AND Jason. Jason always find new things and places to take me. Jason holds my hand all the time whereever we go. Jason tells me he appreciates and loves me every day. The best part he calls me his queen often, he tells me good morning and good night everyday.

Since this was my first time in Denver he wanted to show me different places and sights. Last week Jason took me to the Civic Center, which holds a public library, art museum, the Greek Amphitheater, Pioneer Monument and the Veteran's Memorial. We had so much fun walking around talking with each other and holding hands the whole time.

Jason wanted to take me to as much as he can every week like next weekend he made plans to take me to the Denver Art Museum and to dinner. Jason has already made reservations for the Indian Springs Resort in Idaho Springs. There is so much that Jason wants to do with me that he says he can't wait. Jason has been working with his travel agent to find a wonderful one-month get away two weeks in Paris and two weeks in Greece. Once the agent can have all of the information he asked for then we will go away for a month.

Jason loved the fact that even though I have money that I still watched my pennies and I still looked for the best bargains I can find. I work with 3 special charities that's very special to me. After my procedures I my attitude improved even more than I had after losing my weight. I always knew what I wanted and why. Jason always thought from the moment he saw me that I was beautiful. Jason told me recently that the first time he heard my voice he that it was sexy and he about lost it. Wow I've never heard that before from any man. Jason always would ask me questions that really had nothing to do with my procedures but he wanted to know how I felt about different things and somehow he knew that I was also beautiful on the inside as well.

Jasmine and Jason didn't notice the person following them as they left the restaurant that followed them back to Jasmine's apartment. "Jason what did you think of the house that I rented for the girls weekend, did you like it?" "Jasmine I thought it was great why would you like to live there or maybe a different house?" I think I would love a house one large enough for friends and family to visit." "I think that would be a good idea. How about we go look at houses see if we find anything that we like. If not then we can think about building our dream home." "I love that idea; I can call my real-estate agent that found my apartment tomorrow and tell her we would like to find a house. Jason what do you think the square footage should be?" "Well I think we should look at 3000 square footage at least to 6000 square footage." "I'm in Jason but I would like a ranch style with basement and a high glass ceiling great room I think I would love a mountain or lake view maybe." "Jasmine if it will make you happy then I will be happy you can have whatever you want. I love you."

"Hello this is Michelle" "Hi Michelle it's Jasmine Moore." "Hi Jasmine it's great to hear from you how's the apartment and how did the house work for your girls weekend?" "Michelle it was absolutely wonderful. It worked very well the girls loved it. I also got engaged over the weekend. My finance and I would like to start looking at houses 3000-6000 square feet, ranch style, with either a mountain or lake view." "Wow congratulations Jasmine I'm so happy for you. Tell you what let me start to research some listings for you I have a few places in mind can I give you a call in a day or two and we can set up a time for a showing?" "Sure that is fine Michelle I can't wait to see what you find for us. If we can't find what we want we will look to build." "I'm on it Jasmine I will find you something." Thanks Michelle I have faith in you."

Jasmine what time do we need to be at the house Michelle found for us? 6:00 pm if the map on my phone is correct we have to leave in the next 15 minutes. Jason opened up the car door for me and we headed out to meet Michelle. Jason climbed in behind the wheel. Five minutes into the drive Jason calmly said "Jas I think we have a problem I'm picking up speed and I have no brakes." "What" "I think you better call 911 tell them where we are and that we have no breaks the emergency brake is gone to I'm going to try and find somewhere to hold on." Jason said as he started to honk his horn weaving in and out of light traffic in a hilly area. "Oh my God Jason look out." I said as I was dialing 911." "911 state your emergency." "We have no brakes on our car my fiancé is driving." Mama where are you? "I have no idea Jason what road are we on?" "Hang on I see a high school yard I'm going to try and use to stop." Jason said as he made a sharp turn going over a curb onto the grass of the high school property. "Mama where are you?" I heard the dispatcher say. I was holding on to the door handle and the phone so tightly shaking finally Jason had the car stopped. "Jasmine are you alright?" Jason asked me but I couldn't say anything I still in shock. Jason pulled the phone from my hands and told the dispatcher where we were. "Sir, police and EMS are on their way." "I'm a dr. my fiancé is in shock but we're not injured just shaken up." "Jas honey, please say something." "Jason we could have died what happened. This is a new car there's no recall notice that I know of this Mercedes shouldn't have brake issues.

We could have died." I said again. "Jasmine look at me you're in shock honey. We are both fine just a little shaken but we're fine. Come here let me hold you until EMS get here then we can go to the hospital and have you checked out." "No Jason I just want to go home, crap we have to call Michelle and tell her we need to reschedule." We heard sirens getting closer then we saw the police car with flashing lights. Five minutes later the EMS arrived. Jason and I refused to go to the hospital but I sat in the back of the EMS truck while Jason talked to the police. The techs took all of my vital signs then had me sign a release form. A tow truck arrived to load my car on the bed. There was a little body damage on the finder. The tow truck was taking the car to the dealership so the mechanics could look the car over in the morning and fix the car. The police offered to take us back to the apartment since we were still fairly close.

"Jasmine, I want you to go get comfortable and into bed I will join you shortly. I'm going to lock up the house and set the alarm." I nodded, and walked into the bedroom.

I just finished pulling the sheets back when Jason walked in. "Jasmine are you ok?" "No, I'm not Jason but I will be. Hurry up and come to bed so you can hold me and I can have a good cry." Jason took off his clothes right there and climbed into bed with me. "Come here baby" I had just curled into his arms as the tears started. "Jason I have never been as scared to death as I was tonight. I'm glad you were driving I would not have known what to do. I would have done something wrong and would have hit someone or something." "Jasmine you would have done fine I'm sure of it you're a strong woman."

"Jason do you think we should have all of the cars checked once we get my car back?" "I think that is a good idea Jas

I don't want you to drive any of your cars until we get a report on your car. Call the car service ask for a driver and security person." "What! Why do I need a security guard?" "Jasmine just humor me please I will feel better if you have a driver and a security detail until we find out what happened to your car. I've driven a Mercedes car for a long time and they just don't lose brakes like that and the emergency brakes wouldn't work either."

"Ok Jason I will call tomorrow, I'm not going to go anywhere anyway for a day or two." Jason held me as I cried letting everything go. He held me all night as I slept. The next morning I woke up and found a note on his pillow.

Good morning my Queen. I'm sorry baby I had a surgery this morning and you were resting peacefully. I will call and check on you later. Please stay in today but if you have to go out remember car service and security. Love you, J

Mario and Dan came into the apartment at the same time as I came out of the bedroom. "Jas, what's wrong? You're eyelids are swollen and your eyes are red." "Jason and I had an accident yesterday. The brakes on my car failed and so did the emergency brakes. We had quite the scare on our way to look at a house. My car is at the dealership being looked at." "OMG Jas are you and Jason alright, where is Jason by the way?" "Jason was here with me all night but had a surgery this morning. He's fine I was in shock yesterday. I'm fine now I think. I'm staying home today."

"Ok can I fix you something to eat in the meantime?" "I would love a coffee with a light breakfast? We didn't have dinner last night" "Girl you sit down at the table and I will fix you something."

"Dan, I don't feel up to working out today. Can we hold off a day or two, take one day at a time?" "Jas, you've had a big shock don't worry about working out today or tomorrow but we will get you back into the swing of things soon." "Ok thanks" "in the mean time I will hang out here with you and Mario today. I want to make sure you're ok." "Ok but you really don't have to do that Dan" "I know but I will feel better just looking out for you. You were in shock and may feel like your fine now but you maybe still in shock. Just humor me please." "Alright fine you can stay but I'm really fine." "We will see.

Later that evening Jason came into the apartment. Dan, Mario and I were all siting in the living room watching tv. "Hi Jason, Dan and I stayed to watch out for Jasmine." Dan said to Jason, then Mario stood up. "I held dinner till you got here are you hungry? Jasmine hasn't eaten yet/" "Guys!" "Sorry but we're worried about you." "Dan, Mario I can't say thank you enough for looking out for Jasmine for me. I truly appreciate both of you.

Just then Jason's phone rang. "Hello, yes detective did you find out anything?" Dr. Weston the dealership called us about the break line on Ms. Moore's car. Someone had to have cut the line." "Ok, detective what happens next?"

"Well the dealership will fix the car do you know if the apartment has surveillance cameras?" "I believe they do detective the office manager should be able to confirm that." "Dr. Weston we will continue to investigate the situation. Do you know if someone is stalking Ms Moore or has a grudge?" "No detective I don't" "I would advise if Ms. Moore has any other cars to have them checked out too. I will call Ms. Moore tomorrow to ask more questions." "Detective I'm with her right now if you would like to talk to her." "Thank you Dr. Weston but I will call her tomorrow I have a few more things to check out first before I talk to her. Please let her know I will call her tomorrow afternoon."

Jason got off the phone and told me what detective Robinson said. "Jason what does this all mean that someone is out to get me? Who? I didn't go through my original plan. I called everything off once when my friends where all here. Who would want to either hurt me or kill me/us? Jason I'm scared." "Jasmine I'm getting you a full time body guards. Please don't argue with me about the guards." "Jason I'm not going to argue with you I'm scared enough to agree." Jason held me as I cried.

Jason called Blake a friend of his that is a security specialist to get his input on security for me. Blake came over and did a sweep of my other cars and the apartment. He told us he believed that the other cars brake lines had been cut too. Blake also made suggestions to make the apartment more secure. "Blake I appreciate you coming over tonight.

Would you be able to make all of this happen as soon as possible? I don't care what the cost is, and if you know or recommend body guards I would appreciate it." "Jasmine I will be happy to help you and Jason out. I can have one of my teams here tomorrow afternoon once we pull the right materials to put in the apartment. I can also make some calls tonight and get you a team of body guards." "Oh thank you and thank God."

Blake did everything he said he would and more. Before Blake left he had his team pulled to do a full install the next afternoon and a set of bodyguards to start first thing tomorrow morning.

A week later I found myself relaxing having guards around me. More relaxed having someone drives me around. But also it is a little sad to have to result to having guards. Privacy is not the way that I had before. Even when Jason and I are together we have guards still around inside the apartment they go to another room. We finally rescheduled a house tour with Michelle and had Blake meet us there to talk security. We all discussed if we go with an existing house what changes that we would have to make and how we would either have to take existing room and make changes. Or if we build a home what we can put into the floor plan from the beginning. The discussion went to the electronics and systems that would be needed. I had a question that I wondered and finally asked the room. "What would be the time frame if we buy a house and doing remodel vs. designing and building a house?" "Honestly

Jasmine, if you find an existing house that gives you the square footage you want then it would be easy to remodel it to include your safe room and adding any additional systems and electrical and generators backup systems. I would have 3 total systems one for the security system and the other for the main house. Then the 3rd one is a secured unknown back up to the security like a fail-safe system."

"Ok" as I turned to look at Jason. "Are we on the same page to buy an existing house and remodel?" "Jasmine whatever you want baby." "Ok then Michelle, up the square footage to 6000-8000. That will give us the extra room to put in the safe room and security. If we can find a house that already has something that we can update great. Next we will need an architect to work with Blake to make the changes we want."

The next day Michelle showed Jason, the team and me another house that was had a safe room but needed more security options added. I liked the floor plan and we would not have to do a lot of remodeling. I would have to get my interior designer to help with the remodeling plan and updating the wall colors. I went outside the patio doors and saw a wonderful mountain view in the background and a beautiful back yard with a small creek on the property. This property was on 10 acres and was 9500 square feet. There was also a pool and pool house and a small shed that could be updated to house the backup generators. I was standing there and Jason came up and wrapped his arms around me.

Then we heard a noise rang out but what was it. Before I knew what was happening the security team was running out and Jason and I was. Oh what was that I had a pain in my chest I was going down and so was Jason to the ground. Man why is my chest on fire. "Jasmine are you alright?" I went to say something but couldn't get anything to come out. "Oh call 911 she's been hit" I looked over to see Jason by me but he was hit and bleeding too. I raised my hand to him and the security guard saw that Jason was bleeding. "Jason lay down your bleeding too. Let's get them secured." Tears started to run down my eyes. "Jasmine, stay with me, don't you dye on our watch. Get me something to try and stop the bleeding." I think that was Clark the body guard that was teamed up with Trinity and Nathan today. Damn I'm hurting and oh and I passed out. "We're losing here start CPR Trinity until EMS get here."

Finally the man thought as he was watching and listening from his hiding place. He acted on a spur of the moment seeing they were touring another house that gave him an advantage. Jasmine will have to die for his plan to work.